"I saw something," said Wyatt. "Is that a stuffed pig? Because stuffed animals are for loser babies."

"It's not a stuffed animal!" I cried. "It's a . . . a lunch bag."

"You talk to your lunch?" Wyatt asked.

"Only when it's bologna," I said.

Also by Katherine Applegate

The One and Only Ivan

ROSCOE RILEY RULES

#2 Never Swipe a
Bully's Bear

Katherine Applegate
illustrated by Brian Biggs

HARPER

An Imprint of HarperCollinsPublishers

For Jessie and her mom and dad

Roscoe Riley Rules #2: Never Swipe a Bully's Bear
Text copyright © 2008 by Katherine Applegate
Illustrations copyright © 2008 by Brian Biggs

Library of Congress Cataloging-in-Publication Data
Applegate, Katherine.
Never swipe a bully's bear / Katherine Applegate ; illustrated by
Brian Biggs. — 1st ed.
       p.   cm.
ISBN 978-0-06-239249-7
Summary: When first-grader Roscoe discovers that his stuffed pig is
missing from his backpack, he accuses the class bully of "pig-napping"
and gets even by taking the bully's teddy bear.
[1. Toys—Fiction. 2. Lost and found possessions—Fiction.
3. Bullies—Fiction. 3. Schools—Fiction.] I. Humorous stories.
PZ7.A6483 Nes 2008   2007033412
[Fic]   CIP
                                                                AC

Typography by Jennifer Heuer
15 16 17 18 19 OPM 10 9 8 7 6 5 4 3 2 1
❖
Revised paperback edition, 2015

#2

Never Swipe a
Bully's Bear

Contents

1

Welcome to Time-Out

Welcome to the Official Roscoe Riley Time-out Corner.

It's nice to have some company.

Getting stuck in time-out can be awfully boring.

Thing is, I got in a teensy bit of trouble. Again.

1

Even though I really, truly didn't mean to.

You know, it's hard for a guy like me to keep track of so many rules.

So I've started keeping a list.

This time I broke rule number 214: Do not kidnap your classmate's teddy bear.

And hide him in the dirty clothes basket.

Who knew?

You've bear-napped before, right?

Oh.

Bunny-napped? Pig-napped? Kangaroo-napped?

Oh.

Well, looking back, I guess it *does* seem like a bad idea.

But maybe you'll understand better if I tell you the whole story. . . .

2

Something You Should Know
Before We Get Started

You are never too old to love a stuffed animal.

I'll bet one of your favorite grown-ups has an old teddy bear hidden in a closet.

And I'll bet it has a silly name too.

Like Hugaboo. Or Mr. Tickletoes. Or Poopzilla.

Why do people always give their stuffed animals such crazy names?

Search me. I named my stuffed pig Hamilton.

He is way too cool to be called Poopzilla.

3

Something Else You Should Know
Before We Get Started

I don't care what you've heard.

Hamilton does NOT wear dresses.

4

Hamilton

I wouldn't be stuck here in time-out if I'd just listened to my big brother.

And believe me, I hardly ever say that.

It started the other day. I was packing Hamilton into my backpack.

So he could go to school with me. Just like always.

Max saw me. "No pigs allowed at school, Roscoe," he said.

I ignored him.

Because number one, that isn't a rule. Unless the pig is the real kind.

And number two, when a little brother ignores a big brother, it drives the big brother crazy.

Max was eating Cheerios. He threw one at my head. "You're in first grade now," he said. "And first graders do NOT take stuffed animals to school."

I picked the Cheerio out of my hair.

Then I ate it.

That also drives big brothers crazy.

"Hamilton always comes with me," I said.

Mom ran into the kitchen. "Has anyone seen Hazel's Cinderella toothbrush?"

Hazel is my little sister. She has a thing about princesses. Also mud.

"The point is, stuffed animals are for babies," Max said.

"Max!" Mom said. "What are you talking about?"

"Roscoe's taking that stinkpot Bacon to school," Max said.

"That isn't his name," I said.

"Ham," Max said.

"Ham-ILTON," I said.

"It would be totally embarrassing if anyone sees you with that thing," Max said. "I'd be humiliated!"

"You are in fourth grade," Mom said. "Roscoe's in first. How is he going to humiliate you?"

Max shook his head. "I'm sorry, Mom," he said, "but you know nothing about the real world. People will talk."

"That pig is Roscoe's best friend," Mom said. "And as long as it's okay with his teacher, he may take Bacon—I mean

Hamilton—to school."

"Besides, nobody knows he's there," I pointed out. "'Cause he stays in my backpack. Only Emma and Gus know about him. And Ms. Diz."

Ms. Diz is my teacher. And Emma and Gus are my best buddies.

Max made a pig-snort sound.

I snorted back. Twice.

Let me tell you, dealing with big brothers is an art.

"I'm bringing Hamilton," I said. "And that's that."

The thing is, I've had Hamilton forever.

My Great-aunt Hilda sent him to me on my first birthday.

She has a pig farm in North Carolina.

Great-aunt Hilda says pigs are very intelligent and lovable.

Sort of like snorting dogs.

I can't sleep without Hamilton.

When I was little, he kept away monsters and fire-breathing dragons.

When I got bigger, he kept away black widow spiders and grizzly bears.

He is my guard pig.

"Guys!" Dad called. "Hustle! It's almost time for the bus!"

Max ran to get his backpack. Mom ran to find Hazel's toothbrush.

I sat in the kitchen and stared at Hamilton.

I put him on the counter.

What if Max was right?

I was getting awfully old.

I mean, I had a loose tooth. That's WAY old.

Hamilton looked worried, like he might start to cry.

I could see this was very hard for him.

"Okay, buddy, you can come," I said.

I smushed Hamilton into the very bottom of my backpack.

I left the zipper open a little. So he could breathe.

Max was crazy. Nobody would bug me about Hamilton.

Because nobody knew about him. Except Ms. Diz and Emma and Gus.

I peeked into my backpack.

"Hamilton," I said. "You can come to school with me forever. Even when I'm a fourth grader."

5

Your Epidermis
Is Showing

When I got to school, I went straight to the cubbies by our classroom.

While I hung up my backpack, I checked to make sure no one was nearby.

Good. The coast was clear.

I whispered to Hamilton through the zipper hole. "See you, buddy."

I heard someone behind me. So I zipped up my backpack really quick.

My pal Gus ran up. His cubby is right next to mine.

Gus's cubby sign looks like this:

GUS CARR

My cubby sign looks like this:

ROSCOE RILEY

I have smaller letters on account of my name is longer.

We headed into the classroom. Emma ran over to join us.

Wyatt zoomed past us, pretending to be a jet.

"Hey, Gus," he yelled. "Your epidermis is showing."

Gus looked worried.

"*Epidermis* just means *skin*, Gus," I told him. "That is the oldest joke on the planet."

I know this because I have a big brother.

Max is useful for some things.

Wyatt zoomed back again.

"Hey, Roscoe," he said, "your proboscis is showing."

That was a new one. Even Max had never said it.

I checked for boogers. I checked my zipper. I checked every other embarrassing thing I could think of.

Emma made an I-don't-know-what-Wyatt's-talking-about face. And she knows lots of big words.

Wyatt laughed a loud, meanish laugh.

My dad says every classroom has a bully.

In Ms. Diz's class, his name is Wyatt.

Dad says when somebody like Wyatt teases you, a good answer is "So what?"

They never quite know what to say to that one.

This also works on little sisters and big brothers.

Feel free to borrow "So what?" anytime you need it.

"I see Roscoe's proboscis!" Wyatt yelled.

"So what?" I said.

Wyatt stopped zooming. He scrunched up his face.

"I'll bet you don't even know what that is," he said at last.

"Do so," I said.

"What is it then?" he said.

"Just zip it, Wyatt," said Emma.

That's a fancy way of saying BE QUIET.

Emma has a way with words.

Suddenly I remembered that I'd zipped up poor Hamilton. How would he breathe without an air hole?

"I'll be right back," I said.

I ran to the cubbies in the hall. No one was there.

I unzipped my backpack. So Hamilton could have some nice, fresh air.

I reached in to move him around. So he could be more comfortable.

"Now you look comfy," I said.

"Who are you talking to, Riley?" someone asked.

I smushed Hamilton down and spun around.

Wyatt!

"Nobody," I said. "I mean, I was just talking to myself."

Wyatt took a step closer. "What's in there, anyway?"

I could feel my face getting red. I hate that.

It's like your epidermis is tattling on you.

"I saw something," said Wyatt. "Is that a stuffed pig? Because stuffed animals are for loser babies."

"It's not a stuffed animal!" I cried. "It's a . . . a lunch bag."

"You talk to your lunch?" Wyatt asked.

"Only when it's bologna," I said.

Which I thought was a pretty good answer.

I walked back into class.

Wyatt was shaking his head.

And staring at my backpack.

6

The Case of the Missing Pig

That night, after I brushed my teeth and put on my pajamas, I went down to the kitchen.

I grabbed my backpack off the counter. I reached inside to pull out Hamilton. But there was an empty space where Hamilton was supposed to be.

WHERE WAS HAMILTON????

I yelled. "HE'S GONE! HAMILTON IS GONE!!!"

Mom and Dad ran in. "Roscoe," Mom said, "what's wrong, honey?"

"HAMILTON IS MISSING I KNOW HE WAS IN HERE AND NOW HE IS GONE WHERE COULD HE BE???!!!" I screamed. "HAMILTON IS LOST!!!!"

I am not always calm in a crisis.

Not when it's about my pig.

"Can you think where you might have left him?" Mom asked.

"If I knew where I'd left him, then he wouldn't be lost!" I cried.

"Did you take Hamilton out for show-and-tell?" Dad asked.

"No way," I said. "Max said I would humiliate him if people knew I brought

Hamilton to school."

"So nobody saw you with the pig?" Max asked.

"Well," I said, "Wyatt saw me talking to him."

"I didn't know you spoke Pig," Max said.

I didn't answer. On account of I was ignoring Max.

"Wyatt is a real pain," I reminded Dad.

"Want me to talk to him?" Max said. "I could threaten to lock him in the boys' room."

"Max!" Mom said. "Don't even think such a thing!"

"A minute ago you were teasing Roscoe," said Dad. "And now you're trying to protect him?"

Max made his shoulders go up and

down. "It's my job, Dad. I'm his big brother."

We looked everywhere for Hamilton.

Under the couch. In the laundry room. In the toy chest. In the garage.

I even checked the bathtub.

Everybody tried to find Hamilton. Even our dog, Goofy.

He could tell we were looking for something.

So he brought us a slobbery tennis ball. A dirty sock. And a Lincoln Log he'd chewed on.

But no Hamilton.

Finally, Mom said, "I'm afraid we have to call it quits for tonight. Hamilton will show up, honey. He's just a very good hider."

We headed upstairs. I climbed into bed.

"My bed feels funny without Hamilton," I said.

Mom tucked the covers around me. "We'll find him, sweetheart," she said. "But for tonight, what could we do to make it easier to sleep?"

I stared at the ceiling. I have a mobile hanging there. It glows in the dark.

It's all the planets. Except Pluto. Which Goofy ate.

I guess that's okay. Since the science guys decided Pluto's not really a planet.

"There's nothing we can do," I said. "I can't sleep without Hamilton. Period. End of story. No more discussion."

Mom says that a lot.

You can pick up some really useful

sayings from adults.

Hazel came into my room.

She was wearing her Pretty Prancing Pony pajamas. With footies.

"Sweetie, you're supposed to be asleep," Mom said.

"I brought something for Roscoe," Hazel said. She held up one of her Barbie dolls.

The doll was wearing an astronaut helmet.

And a white doctor coat.

And purple sparkle high heels.

"Her name is Janelle," Hazel said.

She lay Janelle on my pillow.

It felt all wrong to see that sparkly astronaut doctor lying on Hamilton's favorite spot.

"You can borrow her," said Hazel. "Since you losted Hamilton."

"I didn't lose him!" I shouted. My voice was pretty grouchy. "He disappeared!"

"Roscoe, Hazel is just trying to help," Mom said.

I felt a little bad. Especially because Janelle is Hazel's favorite Barbie.

"Thanks, Hazel," I said. "You're a good sister." I picked up Janelle. Even though I really didn't want to.

She had pointy little hands.

Hamilton had nice soft piggy paws.

"Remember that Janelle likes to sleep with her high heels on," Hazel said.

She sounded a little worried.

"You know what?" I said. "I think Janelle would miss you." I handed Janelle back to Hazel. "She probably wouldn't be able to sleep. But thanks, Hazel."

Hazel grinned. "Yeah, you're probably right. Janelle is very picky."

Mom kissed the top of my head. "Sleep tight, Pumpkin. Hamilton will turn up, I'm sure of it."

After they left, I stared up at my glow-in-the-dark planets.

There was a big, empty spot next to me.

Right where Hamilton was supposed to be.

He snores a little, but that's okay.

Because all pigs do.

The planets swirled softly over my head.

Usually Hamilton and I loved to watch them.

But tonight all I could think about was Pluto.

The missing planet.

7

Pig-Napper!

"Roscoe, you look terrible," said Emma the next morning at school.

"REALLY terrible," Gus agreed.

"I had bad dreams all night," I said. "I dreamed I was a giant pig. And I got locked in a suitcase. And sent to Alaska."

"Alaska, huh?" Emma said.

"I think it was Alaska. 'Cause there were

polar bears and giraffes."

I felt my eyes getting wettish.

Which is not okay when you are an official first grader.

"I can't find Hamilton," I said. "I brought him to school yesterday just like always. And when I got home, he was vanished!"

"Wow," said Gus. "Pig-napping is a serious crime."

"Pig-napping?" I cried. "You mean someone stole him?"

"We don't know if he was pig-napped," Emma pointed out. "Maybe Roscoe left him somewhere. Did you take him to the boys' room?"

When you have a big problem, it is nice to have a good thinker like Emma around.

I shook my head.

"The lunchroom?" Emma asked.

I shook my head harder.

"Did you show him to anyone?" Emma asked.

I thought for a second. "Just Wyatt. I didn't mean for him to see us. But he did. Hamilton was in my backpack. I was just saying a quickie hi."

We all looked over at Wyatt. He was in the activity center making a magnet building.

He saw us looking at him. He pulled on his nose to make a pig face.

"Wyatt isn't my favorite person," Emma said. "He isn't even my tenth favorite person."

"Maybe Wyatt knows what happened to Hamilton," Gus said.

I thought about that. Wyatt was a meanie.

And he'd seen me with Hamilton.

And now Hamilton was missing.

"You don't think . . . Wyatt's a pig-napper, do you?" I whispered.

"Wyatt? Why would Wyatt pig-nap Hamilton?" Gus asked. "I was thinking maybe Mr. McGeely took him."

"Mr. McGeely?" I repeated. "You mean the janitor? You think Mr. McGeely put Hamilton IN THE TRASH?"

"No offense, Roscoe," Gus said. "But Hamilton is kind of, well, old."

"And he smells a little . . . funny," Emma added.

"My Great-aunt Hilda is old and smells funny, and I love her," I said.

Emma smiled. "You're a good guy, Roscoe."

"You know what I'm going to do?" I said. "I'm going to march right over there. And I'm going to ask Wyatt if he took my pig."

But before I could do that, Ms. Diz rang her gonger. It is a big round golden thing shaped like a plate. It hangs from a hook on the ceiling.

When you hit it with a hammer, it goes

g-o-o-n-n-g-g!!!

That means FREEZE!

Ms. Diz used to ring a teensy little silver bell.

But then she figured out we could make more noise than any old bell.

So she outsmarted us. With her giant gonger.

Ms. Diz is a brand-new teacher.

But she is learning fast.

"Time for morning meeting, folks," said Ms. Diz.

We sat in our spots.

We talked about the weather. (Cold.)

We talked about the day. (Tuesday.)

We talked about talking. (We had been

interrupting Ms. Diz a lot.)

She said that when someone is talking, you listen with your ears.

And save your questions for the end.

Then you use your mouth.

Even if you see something that is a miracle.

Like a squirrel with a blue Matchbox car in his mouth.

Which I saw yesterday.

You are not allowed to jump up and scream, "MS. DIZ I SEE A SQUIRREL WITH A MATCHBOX CAR IN HIS MOUTH OR MAYBE IT'S AN SUV!!! I AM NOT KIDDING MS. DIZ!!"

That's just a for-instance.

After we talked about the weather and the day, we read our morning message. Ms. Diz writes it on a giant piece of paper.

It said:

> We have art this afternoon with
> Ms. Large.
> Tomorrow is Hassan's birthday.
> Today Wyatt is our line leader.

I looked over at Wyatt.

He pulled up his nose to make another pig face.

That did it. I jumped up.

I put my hands on my hips. Like a superhero.

"WHAT HAVE YOU DONE WITH MY PIG?" I screamed.

Everybody froze. They were perfectly quiet.

So that when I also screamed, "YOU, SIR, ARE A PIG-NAPPER!" my very loud voice seemed extra especially loud.

"I AM NOT A PIG-NAPPER!" Wyatt screamed back.

He looked at Ms. Diz. "What's a pig-napper, Ms. Diz?"

"Roscoe and Wyatt!" said Ms. Diz. "First of all, sit down, please. Secondly, if you have something to say, you raise your hand."

I raised my hand. I waved it back and forth. Fast as Goofy's tail when he sees my mom with a can opener.

"Yes, Roscoe?" said Ms. Diz.

I looked at Wyatt. "You, sir, are a pig-napper," I said in a nice, gentleman voice.

Wyatt raised his hand. He waved it like a flag on a super windy day.

"Yes, Wyatt?" said Ms. Diz. She looked a little tired. And it was still morning.

"I am not a pig-napper," Wyatt said in a

nice, gentleman voice. "And what exactly is a pig-napper?"

"A pig-napper is a person who takes another kid's most favorite pig out of his backpack when he isn't looking!" I said.

Wyatt rolled his eyes. "Why would I want your stupid stuffed animal? Stuffed animals are for loser babies. I did not take your stinky pig!"

"Prove it!" I screamed.

"You prove it!" Wyatt said. "You 'cused me!"

I ran to Wyatt's cubby. I grabbed his backpack and came back extra fast.

"Roscoe," said Ms. Diz. "This isn't appropriate behavior."

Wyatt jumped up. He grabbed the other side of his backpack.

It said WYATT on it with a picture of a dinosaur.

Wyatt looked pretty mad. Kind of like the *Tyrannosaurus rex* on his backpack.

But I just knew Hamilton was in that backpack.

So I kept pulling.

Ms. Diz came over. She pulled on the backpack straps.

All the kids watched. It was like tug-of-war.

Three ways.

"Boys, let go," said Ms. Diz.

Ms. Diz was using her Listen-or-Else Voice.

Wyatt let go.

So did I.

Ms. Diz fell backward.

She landed—*plop!*—in her teacher chair.

The backpack flew into the air.

Something popped out.

Something stuffed.

But it wasn't Hamilton.

8

Bobo

There on the ground sat a dirty yellow teddy bear. With only one ear.

"BOBO!" Wyatt cried.

He grabbed that bear and hugged it.

"You said only babies have stuffed animals," I said.

"Loser babies," Gus pointed out.

Wyatt's face got very pink.

He dropped that old bear on the ground.

"That's my little brother's bear," Wyatt said, very fast. "I don't know how he got in my backpack!"

But I could tell Wyatt was fibbing.

He had hugged that bear like he really meant it.

. . .

After that we had to go to Mr. Goose-garden's office.

He is the principal. That means he talks to you about your Bad Choices.

I think he is also the boss of the teachers.

Maybe they have to talk to Mr. Goosegarden about their Bad Choices too.

Mr. Goosegarden has a very cool office.

He has a zillion windup toys on his desk.

There is a monkey who does a backflip.

A caterpillar who tap-dances.

A gorilla who pounds his chest.

And teeth that chatter.

The secretary, Mrs. LaBella, led us into Mr. Goosegarden's office. While we waited for him to come in, I wound up the chattering teeth.

Wyatt wound up the gorilla.

We didn't talk to each other.

But we let the toys fight it out on the floor.

Mr. Goosegarden entered. He did not seem surprised to see the teeth and the gorilla fighting.

He sat down and rubbed his eyes and

talked to us about our noisiness.

And about blaming someone without any proof.

And about Bobo and Hamilton.

"Boys," he said, "I'll tell you a little secret. I still have my old teddy bear." He smiled. "And sometimes I even sleep with him."

We were very quiet.

Since this was shocking news.

"No way," I said.

"No way," Wyatt said.

"Way," Mr. Goosegarden said.

Then he made us shake hands.

And pull the chattering teeth off the gorilla.

. . .

We walked back to class, Wyatt and me.

We didn't talk. Because I was still sure Wyatt had my pig.

Well, *pretty* sure.

Also because now everybody knew about Hamilton.

Of course, everybody knew about Bobo, too.

All the way back to our classroom, I thought about poor lonely Hamilton.

Who would tell him funny stories?

Who would rub his tummy?

Who would hug him when he was sad? Who else could have pig-napped him? Except Wyatt?

It was exactly the kind of thing a bullyish guy like Wyatt would do.

We got to the classroom door. Wyatt's backpack was in his hallway cubby.

Bobo's dirty ear was sticking out.

It wasn't fair for Wyatt to have his stuffed animal, when I didn't have mine.

We headed into the classroom. I sat down at one of the worktables.

Emma and Gus sent me sorry-about-the-principal-visit looks.

Ms. Diz rang her gonger.

"We've had some talk today about how

stuffed animals are just for little children," she said.

"Loser babies," Gus corrected.

"Thank you, Gus," said Ms. Diz. "Next time, please raise your hand first."

Ms. Diz went to the blackboard. She wrote:

STUFFED ANIMAL PARTY!

"I would like each of you to bring a favorite stuffed animal to school the day after tomorrow. I think you'll see that all of us have an animal who's very special."

"Even you, Ms. Diz?" Moira asked.

"Even me." Ms. Diz smiled. "And Mr. Goosegarden."

All the kids laughed. Except me.

"Roscoe, I know that you'll be missing

Hamilton if he hasn't turned up by then,"
Ms. Diz said. "But do you have some other
special animal you could bring?"

I sighed. "If I can't have Hamilton, Ms.
Diz," I said, "then I don't want anyone."

I looked over at Wyatt.

He and Bobo were going to have fun
together at the party.

While I would be sad and lonely. And
so would Hamilton.

It wasn't fair.

Then I had an idea.

I wasn't going to be the only person
without his favorite stuffed animal.

9

Welcome to
the Dirty
Clothes Basket

All day long my tummy felt throw-uppy.

Like it does when we go on a family trip. And there are twisty roads.

I hardly ever actually throw up.

But I make the other people in the car pretty nervous.

When Max and me got off the bus,

Mom was in the yard with Hazel.

"How was school, Max?" Mom asked.

"Okay," he said.

"How was school, Roscoe?" Mom asked.

"Okay," I said.

"What did you do today?" Mom asked.

"Nothing," Max said.

"I did nothing too, Mommy," said Hazel, who just goes to preschool half a day.

"What did you do, Roscoe?" asked Mom.

"Nothing," I said.

Because that's what you always say.

Except secretly I was thinking, *Nothing, unless you count bear-napping.* Which is what I did during lunch when no one was looking. I had grabbed that old bear out of Wyatt's backpack and stuck him into mine.

I took off my backpack. I'd left the zipper open halfway.

One little black eye
was staring at me.

One little black,
mad, sad eye.

Just then, I
remembered about
the party.

"Ms. Diz is
making us have
a stuffed animal
party the day
after tomorrow.
So we can see
that animals aren't
just for loser babies,"
I said.

"Maybe you could
bring Geraldo," Mom
said.

"I thought about that," I said. "But if Hamilton can't come, then I'm not bringing anybody else. If he found out, it would hurt his feelings."

I took my backpack to my room.

Bobo looked all squished. Plus he had some peanut butter on his right paw.

"I'm really sorry about this, Bobo," I said. "It's only for a little while."

I sat on my bed. Bobo leaned on my pillow.

He was not smiling at all.

He looked sort of down in the dumps.

"See, your owner took my pig," I said to Bobo. "At least, I'm pretty sure he did. And so if I take you, then Wyatt will see how I feel and then he'll give Hamilton back and then I'll give you back."

I tucked Bobo under the covers.

All of a sudden I thought of Mom tucking me in.

She would see Bobo. And she would ask me where he came from.

"Roscoe," she would say, "I don't believe I've met this guy."

I would have to admit I was a bear-napper.

And I was almost positive for sure that Mom would not approve.

I pulled Bobo out of bed.

I searched around my room for a good hiding place.

I put Bobo in my dirty clothes basket. All kinds of things like to hide in there.

Right under my very muddy jeans.

Hazel and I were playing dinosaur digger-upper that day.

Bobo peeked one sad eye out from under my jeans.

Plus his one ear.

He was lonely. I could tell.

It was hard to figure how he could miss that mean old Wyatt.

I got my armadillo, Geraldo. He was napping under my bed.

"Bobo," I said, "allow me to introduce Geraldo."

I tucked Geraldo in next to Bobo.

I closed my closet door.

At least Bobo would have some company tonight.

Unlike me and Wyatt.

10

Plum

When I woke up the next morning, there was a wet Wheaties flake on my nose.

Max was standing by my bed. Holding a bowl of cereal.

He tossed another Wheaties flake at me.

I sat up and ate it.

"Dad told me to wake you up," Max said.

I yawned. "I couldn't sleep last night."

"How come?" Max asked.

I pointed to my closet. "I think maybe there's a ghost in there," I said.

"Cool," Max said. He slurped down more cereal.

"Max," I said, "did you ever do anything bad so that something good would happen?"

"Sure," Max said. "But the bad part always catches up with you. And then Dad and Mom make you sweep out the garage as punishment."

I pulled the covers over my head. Sometimes big brothers really are right about stuff.

Max yanked all the covers off me.

Sometimes big brothers are right. But mostly they're just really annoying.

. . .

At recess I didn't feel like playing.

Even though Gus found a dead toad with its guts gooing out.

Which usually I wouldn't want to miss, of course.

I sat on a swing. But I didn't actually swing.

Down on the other end of the swing set,

Wyatt was also not swinging.

Ms. Diz came over. She was wearing a pink-and-green scarf.

"Look at you two," she said. "You both seem awfully glum."

"Plum?" I repeated.

"Glum," Ms. Diz said. "Sad."

"I miss Bobo," Wyatt said. "When I got home yesterday, he was missing from my backpack. Just like Hamilton!"

"I miss Hamilton," I said back.

I gave him a look that said *pig-napper*.

"My goodness," said Ms. Diz. "We're having quite an epidemic of disappearing animals!"

She looked at me. Then she looked at Wyatt.

Then she looked at both of us and shook her head.

Wyatt just sat there.

He didn't even have the heart to say a mean bully thing.

He looked like I felt.

Which was awfully plum.

. . .

The next morning was party day.

But I was not feeling at all party-ful.

I still did not have Hamilton back.

And I still *did* have Bobo.

"Roscoe?" Mom said as I headed out

the door. "Are you sure you don't want to bring Geraldo to school today?"

"Nope," I said. "Armadillos are not really party animals, Mom."

As we walked toward the bus stop, I heard Max calling my name.

"Hey, Roscoe," he yelled. "Heads up!"

I turned around. Something blue and floppy was flying through the air.

I caught it.

It was a blue, dirty, droopy dog.

"Who's this?" I asked. "He looks kind of familiar."

Max ran up to join me. "That's my dog. Blueberry."

He unzipped my backpack. "Quick, put him in here before the bus comes."

I squinted my eyes. "Wait a minute. You said you don't have a stuffed animal."

Max shrugged and said, "Roscoe, Roscoe, Roscoe. When are you going to learn? You should only believe your big brother half the time."

"Thanks, Max."

I tried to give him a hug. He yanked away.

"Bus, Roscoe," Max said. "Where's your pride, kid?"

I opened my zipper. "So he can breathe," I explained.

Max grinned. "You're all right," he said. "For a weenie."

. . .

Blueberry fit in with all the other animals.

Emma brought her gorilla.

Gus brought a stuffed snake. It was maybe six feet long.

Wyatt brought a white bunny. He said

he borrowed it from his brother.

That bully boy still looked pretty sad.

Ms. Diz even brought a stuffed animal. It was a kangaroo. And was that guy ever old!

He had patches. He was missing one eye. And his tail was all tattered. From a bad washing machine experience.

Mr. Goosegarden showed up with his old stuffed bear.

We sat in a circle and told about our animals.

Everybody looked a little embarrassed at first.

But before long we were all having fun.

It made me sad to think that Hamilton was missing out.

He loves a good party.

I had a feeling Wyatt was missing Bobo, too.

It turned out we all had favorite animals.

We slept with them.

And drooled on them.

And told them our troubles.

Because whether they were snakes or dogs or teddy bears or porcupines, they were all very good listeners.

11

A Very Unusual Football

"Cheer up, Roscoe," said Emma on the bus that afternoon.

"I'll bet Hamilton is just playing hide-and-seek," said Gus. "A really, really long game of hide-and-seek."

Some kids in the middle of the bus were throwing a football back and forth.

"No throwing things!" shouted the bus driver.

"Or maybe he went on a trip," said Emma.

"Yeah," said Gus. "Maybe he's flying around the world. He could be anywhere by now!"

I sighed.

The ball flew past us.

It was big and pink. And fluffy.

It was for sure not a football.

"Touchdown!" yelled one of the kids.

"No football on the bus!" yelled the driver.

"That's not a football," Emma pointed out. "It's fuzzy. And it's wearing a dress."

I looked.

I swallowed.

I jumped right out of my seat.

Even though that's a really bad idea on a bus.

"THAT'S NOT A FOOTBALL! THAT'S MY PIG!!!" I screamed.

The throwing stopped.

The kids stopped.

The BUS stopped.

"Excuse me?" said the driver.

"HAMILTON!!!" I ran over as fast as I could.

A little boy was holding him. A kindergartner.

"Here," he said. "You can have him. Truth is, he kind of smells, you know?"

"He's wearing a dress!" I cried.

Poor Hamilton. He looked so embarrassed.

"We thought he was a girl," the boy said.

I hugged that pig and I kissed that pig and I didn't care who saw me.

Then I took off his dress.

I saw Max at the back of the bus. He was shaking his head. And laughing with his friends.

His friends who were way too cool to have stuffed animals.

Then Max looked right at me.

And he gave me a wink that only I could see.

. . .

My dad was working in his attic office when I got home.

I ran straight upstairs and told him the amazing wonderful story of Hamilton's return.

"This little girl found him on the sidewalk!" I said.

"The sidewalk?" Dad said.

"I think maybe he fell out of my back-pack when I was doing somersaults on the way home," I said. "Like this."

I did a quickie somersault example.

I kind of knocked into Dad's trash can.

"Oops," I said. "So the girl said she took Hamilton home. And she named him Darlene."

Dad shook his head. "Poor Hamilton."

"And her mom said Hamilton smelled bad. So she put him in the washing machine. Can you believe it?"

"That must have been scary for Hamilton," Dad said.

"So then the girl put a dress on him. Only her mom said he was still too yucky. Which he is not."

I took a whiff of Hamilton.

He still smelled sort of piggy-flavored.

But soapy too.

I hoped the soapy smell would wear off.

"So then the girl gave Hamilton to her brother to use as a football," I said.

I took a deep breath.

"Period," I said. "End of story. No more discussion."

But it wasn't, not really.

12

Your Proboscis Is Showing Too

I took Hamilton to my room so he could see all his friends.

Everyone wanted to hear his exciting story.

I grabbed Geraldo from my laundry basket so he could welcome his buddy back.

I started to close the closet door. But

something made me stop.

And it wasn't a ghost.

I looked down at the laundry basket.

Two sad black eyes
stared up at me.

Hamilton
and I were
together again,
but Bobo was
still alone.

And I knew
that wasn't right.

. . .

I told Dad all about how I had bear-napped poor Bobo.

It felt good to get that old bear off my chest.

Then Dad and I drove over to Wyatt's house.

On the way, Dad and me talked about jumping to conclusions.

Jumping to conclusions isn't about the fun kind of jumping. Like jumping rope. Or jumping jacks.

Jumping to conclusions is when you decide something before you know all the facts.

Like for instance when you think someone is a pig-napper.

Only they aren't.

We also talked about how you are

innocent until somebody proves you guilty.

Personally, I can see how that idea might come in handy.

Wyatt sure was happy to see Bobo.

I told him I was really sorry I thought he was a pig-napper.

And really sorry I was a bear-napper.

Before I left, I remembered something important I had to ask. "Wyatt?" I said. "What's a proboscis?"

"It's just another name for *nose*," he said. He grinned. "I learned it from my big brother. They're good for some things."

Wyatt gave Bobo a hug. Then he sniffed him.

He squinted his eyes. "You didn't give him a bath, did you?" he asked.

"No!" I said. "I might be a bear-napper. But I would never go that far!"

I sighed. "Somebody did that to Hamilton. They even put a dress on him."

Wyatt shook his head. "Some people have no shame."

13

Good-Bye from Time-Out

So now you know why I'm in time-out.

I broke a rule. Number 214 on my list.

Do not bear-nap.

I also learned that sometimes when people say they're Not Guilty, they might *really* be Not Guilty.

Even if their name is Wyatt.

And I learned what a proboscis is.

One more thing. I learned that it's okay to have a stuffed animal. Even if you're twenty, or sixty-five, or one hundred and one.

It's nice to have someone around who always understands you.

That's why I have Hamilton with me here in time-out. He knows I'm really sorry about all the trouble.

Here come Mom and Dad.

They know I'm sorry too.

I think I'll ask them if they still have any stuffed animals.

If they don't, I just might loan them one of mine.

Just as long as it's not Hamilton.

He's had enough adventures lately.

ROSCOE's
Time-Out Activities!

10 SECRETS ABOUT ME YOU PROBABLY DON'T KNOW

by Me, Roscoe Riley

1. I am afraid of ladybugs.

2. I like to put ketchup on my cereal.

3. I have a pair of lucky Spider-Man underpants.

4. I always throw up on merry-go-rounds.

5. When I grow up I am going to marry Ms. Diz if she is interested.

6. My paper airplanes *always* crash.

7. I have three night-lights.

8. I can wiggle my ears.

9. I enjoy flossing.

10. I am going to keep Hamilton until I am 101 years old.

10 MORE RULES TO LIVE BY

by Me, Roscoe Riley

#18—Don't bowl on the
school bus.

#76—Never take your fish
for a walk.

#103—Don't try to make
ketchup soup.

#34—Never hide a secret extra
dessert in your laundry basket.

#57—Don't yell at your brother
in the library, even if he's being
extra annoying.

#42—Never paint with your mom's makeup.

#26—Don't try to wrestle your pillow.

#88—Never play Frisbee with your dad's old records.

#39—Don't fill your birdfeeder with candy.

#61—Never let your dog bury your sister's toys.

CAN YOU SPOT THE DIFFERENCE?

If you want to stay out of trouble, you need to be able to tell when something's wrong. Try to find the seven things that have changed between these pictures.

DID YOU FIND
THEM ALL?

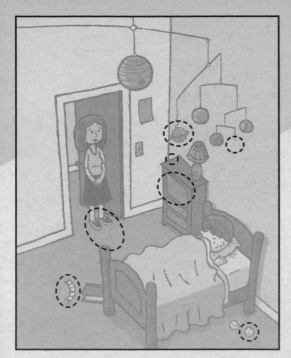

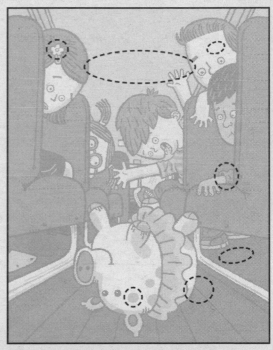

Stuck in time-out again! What went wrong this time?
Read all about my next adventure in

ROSCOE RILEY
RULES

 Don't Swap Your
Sweater for a Dog

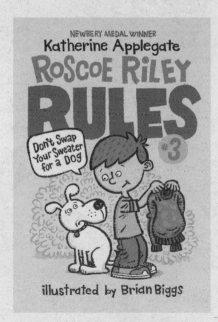

1

Welcome to Time-Out

Hey! Want to play?

Oops. I mean, want to play when I'm done with time-out?

I sort of kind of got in some trouble again.

'Cause I sort of kind of borrowed

somebody's dog.

I only borrowed him so I could win a trophy.

A shiny, sparkly, silver trophy.

You've probably borrowed a dog before, right?

A cat? A gerbil? A tarantula?

Oh. Well, I had my reasons.

It's a long story, actually.

Usually when I end up in time-out, there's a long story to tell.

And since you're here anyway, I'll bet you'd like to hear it. . . .

2

Something You Should Know
Before We Get Started

Just because your dog cannot read a book does not mean he isn't a winner.

Maybe he just hasn't figured out his real talent yet.

3

Something Else You Should Know
Before We Get Started

If your grandma knits you a sweater with pandas and smiley faces and hearts and baby ducks on it, do not give it to Martin.

Or anybody else.

It has sentimental value, you know.

4

The World's Best
Roscoe Riley

This all started because my little sister won another trophy.

Hazel is still in preschool. And she already has a golden trophy from Little Minnows swim team. And one for being the Fastest Skipper in Ms. MacNamara's pre-K class.

So you can see why I was the teensiest bit annoyed when she came home with *another* trophy.

I'd had a long, hard day at school.

On account of an incident involving chocolate milk.

Did you know that if you blow through a straw into chocolate milk, the bubbles will volcano right out of your cup?

The bubbling part is way cool.

Cleaning up the mess afterward is not so cool.

Anyway, after all that, I didn't need to hear Hazel's big news as soon as I opened the door.

"Roscoe!" she screamed. "I wonned another one! For bestest sitting-stiller for the month at circle time!"

"I never got a trophy, and I sit still," I

said. "Well, sometimes I do."

Life is so not fair.

I dropped my backpack in the hall. I kicked off my tennis shoes. Then I flopped on the couch.

"You will not be getting any trophies for neatest boy on planet Earth," Mom said.

"Backpack in the closet. Shoes in your room." She kissed the top of my head.

"I want a trophy," I said in that whining voice you use when you feel really sorry for yourself.

"You got that little plastic statue in kindergarten last year," Mom said. "For most improved hand raising."

"I mean a *real* trophy," I said. "A big, heavy one. Made of gold."

"Shoes," Mom said. "Backpack."

I got off the couch and picked up my shoes and my backpack.

"You are the best burper in first grade," my big brother Max said.

He burped an extra loud one.

It was beautiful. Like music.

"But I'm still the best in the world," Max added.

Which is true. My brother has a gift.

"Everybody's got something cool like a trophy or a statue or something to take to show-and-tell," I said.

"*Every*body?" Mom asked.

"Last week Gus brought his yellow belt from karate," I said. "He got a little gold trophy cup with it. And today Emma brought her piano statue. She got it for practicing lots. It's of that grouchy guy."

"Ludwig van Beethoven," said Mom. "He was a famous music writer."

"Even you have a trophy, Mom," I said. "For selling Girl Scout cookies."

"That was a very long time ago," Mom said. "I was a great little salesperson, though. I could sell snow to a polar bear. I could sell water to an otter. I could sell—"

"Gee, Mom," I interrupted. "You are

big-time not helping me feel better. Which is sort of your job, after all."

Mom gave me a hug. "Sorry, sweetheart. You just be the very best Roscoe you can be. That's all that matters."

Easy for you to say, I thought. *You have a cookie trophy.*

Nobody gives a trophy for being The World's Best Roscoe Riley.

Turn the page for a super-special look at
The One and Only Ivan, winner of the Newbery Medal
and a #1 *New York Times* bestseller!

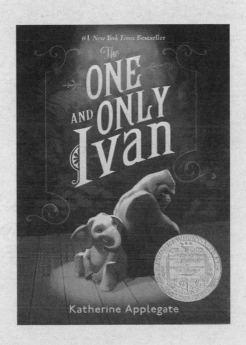

hello

I am Ivan. I am a gorilla.

It's not as easy as it looks.

People call me the Freeway Gorilla. The Ape at Exit 8. The One and Only Ivan, Mighty Silverback.

The names are mine, but they're not me. I am Ivan, just Ivan, only Ivan.

Humans waste words. They toss them like banana peels and leave them to rot.

Everyone knows the peels are the best part.

I suppose you think gorillas can't understand you. Of course, you also probably think we can't walk upright.

Try knuckle walking for an hour. You tell me: Which way is more fun?

patience

I've learned to understand human words over the years, but understanding human speech is not the same as understanding humans.

Humans speak too much. They chatter like chimps, crowding the world with their noise even when they have nothing to say.

It took me some time to recognize all those human sounds, to weave words into things. But I was patient.

Patient is a useful way to be when you're an ape.

Gorillas are as patient as stones. Humans, not so much.

how I look

I used to be a wild gorilla, and I still look the part.

I have a gorilla's shy gaze, a gorilla's sly smile.
I wear a snowy saddle of fur, the uniform of a
silverback. When the sun warms my back, I cast a
gorilla's majestic shadow.

In my size humans see a test of themselves. They
hear fighting words on the wind, when all I'm
thinking is how the late-day sun reminds me of a
ripe nectarine.

I'm mightier than any human, four hundred
pounds of pure power. My body looks made for
battle. My arms, outstretched, span taller than the
tallest human.

My family tree spreads wide as well. I am a great ape, and you are a great ape, and so are chimpanzees and orangutans and bonobos, all of us distant and distrustful cousins.

I know this is troubling.

I too find it hard to believe there is a connection across time and space, linking me to a race of ill-mannered clowns.

Chimps. There's no excuse for them.

KATHERINE APPLEGATE's favorite stuffed animal when she was a kid was a white dog named Sherpa, who had a funny-looking ponytail on top of his head. Now that she's a grown-up, Katherine has written lots of books for kids, including *The One and Only Ivan*, which was awarded the 2013 Newbery Medal. Katherine lives in Northern California with her husband, two kids, assorted pets, and Sherpa, who is looking a little worn around the edges these days but remains a steadfast friend. You can visit her online at www.katherineapplegate.com.

BRIAN BIGGS has illustrated more than fifty books written by many amazing authors and has written a few books himself. Growing up in Arkansas and Texas, Brian tried really hard to stay out of trouble. He did what his teachers and parents asked, he followed the rules, and he got good grades. Now he lives in Philadelphia with his wife and teenagers, where he spends his days drawing and writing in an old garage where he can pretty much do whatever he wants. You can visit him online at www.mrbiggs.com.

Discover the unforgettable Newbery Medal–winning novel

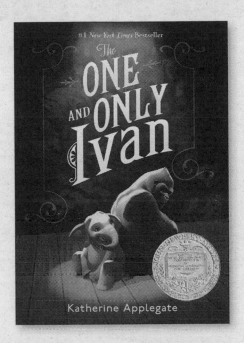

The One and Only Ivan is an uplifting story that celebrates the power of unexpected friendships, told through the eyes of a captive gorilla known as Ivan.

Don't miss the full-color collector's edition of *The One and Only Ivan!*

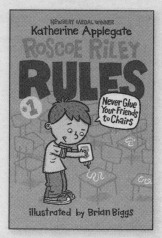